The Mockingbird Files

Satirical Stories for a Witty Mind

Sayan Panda

Ukiyoto Publishing

All global publishing rights are held by

Ukiyoto Publishing

Published in 2024

Content Copyright © Sayan Panda

ISBN 9789362699749
*All rights reserved.
No part of this publication may be reproduced,
transmitted, or stored in a retrieval system, in any form
by any means, electronic, mechanical, photocopying,
recording or otherwise, without the prior permission of
the publisher.*

The moral rights of the authors have been asserted.

*This is a work of fiction. Names, characters, businesses,
places, events, locales, and incidents are either the
products of the author's imagination or used in a fictitious
manner. Any resemblance to actual persons, living or
dead, or actual events is purely coincidental.*

*This book is sold subject to the condition that it shall not by
way of trade or otherwise, be lent, resold, hired out or
otherwise circulated, without the publisher's prior
consent, in any form of binding or cover other than that in
which it is published.*

www.ukiyoto.com

To the one who wants to have a good laugh...

Contents

Forbidden Fruits	1
The Case of the Curious Mr. Roy	6
The Last Birthday Party	12
Bikash Babu's Campaign Story	16
Year 2050	21
The Tale of Two Slanguists	25
How to Procrastinate?	29
The Daily Grind	33
Ghosted	36
Interview	40
About the Author	44

Forbidden Fruits

It was a sunny afternoon and Gunomoy Bagchi was excited to visit the local library, Jubo Shamaj Pathagaar, after his evening classes. As the president of the library council, Gunomoy took pride in the collection they had painstakingly built over decades to cater to the intellectual curiosity of readers from all walks of life in their community.

Gunomoy opened the heavy wooden doors of the library, eagerly greeting his friend Lalmohan, the head librarian. "Any new arrivals I should check out?" he asked eagerly. But Lalmohan's sullen expression gave him pause.

"I'm afraid there have been some...changes during your absence," Lalmohan began hesitantly. "The district administration issued an order last week. They have banned over a hundred books from our shelves."

Gunomoy was aghast. "Banned books? In our library? On what grounds?"

Lalmohan sighed. "The usual vague reasons - objectional content, risk of inciting unrest. But between you and me, I suspect the real reason is to curb free thought."

Gunomoy walked over to the now-empty shelves that used to be filled with books on politics, economics, philosophy and other subjects. "This is an attack on intellect. We cannot let them get away with this travesty!"

From that day on, Gunomoy declared a personal war against the censors. He vowed that the banned books must continue to reach readers, even if secretly. With Lalmohan's assistance, they discreetly maintained a "forbidden catalogue" of the banned titles. If a regular patron inquired about one of the books, Lalmohan would tell them "I'm afraid that book is currently unavailable. But I may know someone who can help you access it elsewhere..." and discreetly pass their name to Gunomoy.

Soon, Gunomoy had assembled an underground network of book smugglers. Under the cover of darkness, books were discreetly passed from house to house, like contraband, until they reached the hands of readers. Gunomoy maintained contacts across the district and beyond, calling in favors to constantly replenish their stock.

One of Gunomoy's most reliable sources was a travelling bookseller named Hiran. During his routes across the country, Hiran would pick up copies of banned titles and, for a small fee, routes them to Gunomoy's secret drop points. It was from Hiran that Gunomoy procured the most controversial title yet - a book that explicitly criticized the policies of the district commissioner himself.

But little did Gunomoy know, a shadowy figure had been watching his activities closely - Radhamohan, a zealous deputy commissioner known for his harsh censorship tactics. Radhamohan had long resented what he saw as the "subversive influence" of Jubo Shamaj Pathagaar. He was determined to bring the maverick library and its meddlesome president down.

One unlucky evening, Hiran was ambushed on his way back from a meeting with Gunomoy. The packets of books were seized and Hiran was arrested. Under interrogation, the terrified bookseller revealed everything - the names of Gunomoy and other members of the underground network.

The next day, Gunomoy arrived at the library as usual, only to find it cordoned off by police. Lalmohan was in custody as well. Before Gunomoy could react, he found himself surrounded by armed police officers. "Gunomoy Bagchi, you are under arrest for illegal possession and distribution of banned literature. You will be tried according to the Defense of India act."

The trial was a mere formality. Radhamohan had stacked the benches with hand-picked judges and witnesses. Gunomoy conducted his own defense passionately, arguing for intellectual freedom. But it was clear the outcome was predetermined. Gunomoy was found guilty and sentenced to two years in prison.

The library too was declared permanently shut down as a "den of anti-national activities". Jubo Shamaj Pathagaar's collections were bonfired publicly, much to the horror of bibliophiles across the district. Radhamohan had achieved total victory over his nemeses. Or so he thought.

In prison, Gunomoy's passion for books and reading only grew stronger. Deprived of access to any texts, he turned to the greatest book of all - his own mind and memories. Every night, he mentally reconstructed plots of his favorite novels, plays, essays. His fellow inmates too looked forward to his "bedtime stories", the only escape from the drudgery of prison life.

But Gunomoy dared to dream even bigger. If books could not come to the people, then the people must have access to books. Once released, he would rebuild the underground network on a massive scale and take the revolution nationwide. No law could stop the free flow of ideas between willing readers and writers. A censored society was one dead in the waters of thought. As long as a single page remained unread, the fight for intellectual freedom was not over.

Two years later, Gunomoy stepped out of prison a free man, but a wanted man. The first thing he did was visit Lalmohan in the hospital. Though frail, the old librarian's passion for books burned as bright as ever. They smiled knowingly at each other, for the real work was only beginning. From the shadows, Gunomoy quietly set the wheels in motion for the greatest book smuguggling operation the world had ever seen. The story does not end here. This is only the beginning of Gunomoy's journey to keep the lamps of free expression burning against the coming darkness. Some battles are won, but the war for independent thought will rage on... as long as there are readers seeking answers beyond what they are told.

The Case of the Curious Mr. Roy

Ritabrata Roy prided himself on being a logical, rational man. As the head of research at a leading analytics firm, he based all his decisions on cold, hard data. Feelings and intuition need not apply in Ritabrata's world.

"Facts don't care about your opinions," was his oft-repeated mantra. Ritabrata lived his life by the numbers - every purchase, relationship and activity was meticulously planned, analyzed and optimized. There was no room for variability or unknown factors in Ritabrata's well-oiled machine of an existence.

His colleagues respected but also feared Ritabrata's laser-like focus and insistence on empiricism. "There he goes again with his spreadsheets," they would joke when Ritabrata pulled out his trusted notebook to crunch numbers on even the most minor decisions.

Though successful in his work, Ritabrata's singular obsession with logic left little room for passion or spontaneity in other parts of his life. Dating was an especially torturous process of rating potentials based on esoteric criteria and number of standard deviations from an algorithmically generated 'ideal partner.' Needless to say, Ritabrata remained happily single and fully in control of his well-ordered domain.

Everything changed one night when Ritabrata's world began unraveling in the strangest of ways. It had been a long day at the office and he was looking forward to a relaxing evening of scheduled recreation activities. But as he walked the five blocks from the subway to his apartment (the most efficient route according to Waze), a strange fog settled over Ritabrata's usually logical mind.

Under the moonlit haze, he found himself drawn to the lively beat spilling out of a corner jazz bar - a musical genre he had previously dismissed as too unstructured and unpredictable in his research. Against all logical consideration, Ritabrata stepped inside for a drink, transfixed by the fluid solos emanating from the stage.

As the notes washed over him, Ritabrata felt an unfamiliar lightness invade his usual rigorously organized mind. A smile played on his lips and his shoulders relaxed from their habitual tension. When an elegant stranger struck up a conversation at the bar, Ritabrata eagerly joined in with no risk-benefit analysis in sight. He found herself sharing personal details and intriguing perspectives without a second thought for optimizing outcomes.

It was as if a different, more carefree person had taken over Ritabrata's logical machinery. By the end of the night, he had not only diverged from his meticulously mapped route home, but also arranged to see his newfound friend again the following week without consulting anyone or anything but the strange feelings stirring within.

The disquieting event shook Ritabrata to his core. Had the carefully constructed walls of reason and order he had built suddenly come crashing down? He replayed the bizarre evening over and over, searching desperately for some logical thread to explain the uncharacteristic behaviors. But try as he might, no amount of data could reconcile the peculiar pull of the music or the mysterious allure of his chance acquaintance.

In the days that followed, more anomalous slip-ups defied Ritabrata's rational control. He found himself stopping to watch street performers instead of briskly adhering to his steps quota. In meetings, previously rigorously-researched opinions gave way to uncharacteristic gut instincts. At a luncheon with investors, he even cracked an impromptu joke that produced startling, unanalyzed laughter.

Ritabrata was losing his grip and it terrified him. Desperate to regain equilibrium, he embarked on an exhaustive self-study, collecting piles of information on abnormal psychology, hypnosis, foreign influence syndromes - anything that could shed light on his disturbing transformation. He became his own case study, meticulously charting and quantifying each uncharacteristic urge or aberrant action.

Still, no amount of research could rationalize how a lifelong skeptic of anything non-empirical had seemingly fallen under some strange, irrational spell. In a last-ditch effort, Ritabrata underwent a battery of medical tests, hoping to uncover some biological culprit for his sudden inability to see the world through only logic and reason. But aside from slightly elevated stress levels, all results came back normal, leaving Ritabrata as baffled as ever.

It was then that a breakthrough came from an unlikely source. In discussing his dilemma with his free-spirited sister, she chuckled and said simply, "It sounds like you could use a vacation, brother! When was the last time you took a break and relaxed without an agenda?"

The suggestion was so foreign to Ritabrata's work-centered existence that he didn't even know how to process it. But with few other options presenting themselves, he reluctantly agreed to take a week off and leave the city, hoping the change of scenery might restore some clarity.

And so Ritabrata found himself in a quaint rural town near the coast, completely outside of his careful calculations and controls. With no schedule to adhere to, he wandered dirt paths seemingly at random, soaking in nature's simplicity. On a whim, he joined locals for homemade meals and stories under the stars.

Slowly but surely, Ritabrata felt the grip of tension ease from his shoulders. Clarity returned not through logic but serenity - an experience so vastly different from his hyper-analyzed existence that it could only be called transcendent. As each day passed freely without the usual frameworks, he saw deeper truths emerge that numbers could never capture.

By the end of his unscheduled sojourn, Ritabrata had undergone a profound inner shift. He returned to the city transformed, still analytical but now with a deeper understanding that both logic and mystery must have their place within. Structure had its uses, but flexibility and wonder were also life's essential ingredients.

From that point on, Ritabrata incorporated more play into his productivity. He pursued passions not out of obligation but enjoyment. And though still data-driven in his work, he came to see the humanity in seemingly illogical behaviors and new perspectives. Most surprisingly of all, that chance jazz bar connection grew into a fulfilling relationship, showing Ritabrata that life's sweetest things often arrive when we least expect or plan for them.

His curious episode had taught Ritabrata the power of stepping beyond reason's constraints to find greater reward. Logic was no longer his sole guiding force, but one philosophical tool among harmony with feelings, spirit and play. Balance was the ultimate principle guiding his enlightened reality. And so the formerly rigid Mr. Roy embraced life's richness in all its perplexing fullness.

The Last Birthday Party

Shashankha woke up on the morning of their 33rd birthday with a growing sense of loneliness and melancholy. They rolled over in their large empty bed and stared at the dust particles floating in through the windows, illuminated by the morning sun. It had been over a year now since the pandemic had swept through the world and claimed the lives of nearly every other human. Shashankha was miraculously spared, though they never figured out why, and now they were left as the sole survivor on the planet.

Every day seemed to blend together into an indistinguishable haze of solitude. Shashankha kept themselves busy with tasks like farming, repairing anything that broke, and scavenging what was left in abandoned buildings, but it did little to lift their constant low mood. As their birthday approached, they decided they had to do something to mark the occasion and celebrate still being alive, if only to stave off the dreariness for a little while.

After eating a meager breakfast by themselves as usual, Shashankha set about preparing for their very first self-birthday party. "This is going to be the event of the century!" they said to the empty room. They dug out the tattered old decorations that they had been hoarding "for a special occasion" and hung up colorful streamers and balloons all around their farmhouse. A hand-drawn banner reading "HAPPY BIRTHDAY SHASHANKHA" was taped up crookedly above the fireplace.

In the backyard, Shashankha assembled a makeshift picnic area under the large oak tree and laid out all the supplies they had scavenged - bags of chips, cans of soda, jars of peanut butter and jams, cartons of cookies. They even baked their favorite vanilla cupcakes from scratch and topped them messily with homemade strawberry frosting. Everything was ready, but there was just one problem - they had no guests to share it with!

Shashankha debated with themselves on what to do. "I guess I'll just have to invite some substitutes," they decided. They walked into town and found an abandoned toy store that was still surprisingly well-stocked. Shashankha gathered an armful of dolls and stuffed animals and brought them back to the party. "Welcome, everyone! I'm so glad you could all make it," they said cheerfully as they arranged their new friends around the picnic area.

The teddy bears just stared glassy-eyed while the dolls said nothing, of course. Shashankha frowned, feeling sillier by the moment. "This isn't really working is it?" they admitted to themselves. They needed real guests, even if they had to use their imagination. Shashankha decided to reenact conversations they used to have with old friends, speaking both parts out loud. It was lonely pretending, but it beat sitting in silence.

As the afternoon wore on, Shashankha got more and more into the roleplaying. Stories and inside jokes from years past flowed effortlessly. For brief moments, they could trick their mind into forgetting they were the only one there. One fake conversation led to another, and before long Shashankha found themselves laughing and crying at different points, reliving treasured memories. The cupcakes sat forgotten, their candles unlit.

Darkness fell and the party drew to a close. Shashankha gathered up the empty dishes and deflated balloons, glancing one last time at the toys who had been such pleasant if imaginary company. Back in their house, a profound sense of loss settled over them once more. They thought of all the real friends and family members they would never see or speak to again. Birthdays would never be the same.

As Shashankha stared into the dying embers of the fire, an idea struck them - if imaginary friends could offer temporary solace, what else could their imagination provide? From that moment on, Shashankha vowed to use their creative powers to try and fill the vast emptiness left by the loss of humanity. They would invent new people to keep them company each day, craft lively stories in their mind, and even re-enact entire scenes from movies they remembered. Anything to keep pushing back the bleak silence.

So every year on their birthday, Shashankha continues this tradition - decorating extravagantly, laying out a wild assortment of food and drink, and pretending as vividly as possible that the party is in full swing. For a brief time, they allow themselves to get completely lost in the fiction and imagine countless imaginary guests chatting and laughing all around. It's the only way now to hold on to that sense of warmth, joy and connection that used to define birthdays past. In their lonely world, imagination and memories are truly the greatest gifts.

Bikash Babu's Campaign Story

Day 1 of Campaigning

Dear Diary,

Today was the first day of my campaign for the big state elections. I decided to start my day with a beautiful morning walk along the river while practising my campaign speech. Everything was going smoothly until I spotted my biggest rival candidate Ambarish Agrawal doing yoga by the river bank. I tried my best to show off in front of him by walking extra fast and even tried some questionable yoga poses. Unfortunately, I fell face-first into a patch of mud within minutes. How embarrassing! I looked like a sad mud-monster when I finally managed to get up. Ambarish and his goons had a good laugh at my expense. I swear I'll get my revenge on that jerk someday. After spending a good hour cleaning up, I finally began my door-to-door campaigning in the nearby villages. The locals weren't very welcoming though. As I explained my vision and policies to them, all I got in return was a "Hmm we'll think about it" or a door shut right in my face. I'm starting to think I picked the wrong career path. Politics is hard work!

Day 2 of Campaigning

Dear Diary,

Today I hired some professional campaign managers to train me on how to better interact with voters. Their first tip - smile more even if you want to strangle someone. That's going to be tough but I'll try my best. My smile muscles were definitely getting a workout during campaigning today. Every time someone said they weren't "fully convinced" by me yet, I gave them my biggest toothy grin and said "no problem, I understand". While this fake cheerful approach was draining, I think some people started warming up to me. Good progress! My managers also told me to carry sweets to distribute. Apparently nothing wins votes like free diabetes. So for the rest of the day, I drove around towns handing out kaju katlis to everyone. Many people who were earlier iffy about me seemed quite happy with the sugar rush I provided. I think my candy strategy might just work! Politics is all about the sweet talk after all.

Day 3 of Campaigning

Dear Diary,

I woke up with a terrible stomach ache today after eating too many of the sweets I was distributing yesterday. Should've practised what I preach - everything in moderation. Feeling under the weather, I decided to host a political rally in the city centre instead of door-to-door campaigning. My managers helped me prepare an energy-packed speech highlighting my vision of developing roads, schools, hospitals etc in the area. I also had some flashy videos and trending slogans ready. The junta seemed quite engaged until torrential rains poured down midway through my speech. In my panic to save the expensive campaign equipment, I slipped on the muddy ground and plopped into a giant puddle, drenching myself from head to toe. The crowd had another good laugh at my expense before scattering away. My dignity and credibility are really taking hits out here. On the bright side, at least the rains have washed away any sticky sweet remnants from yesterday! I'll skip the sugary strategy from now. Back to the drawing board...

Day 4 of Campaigning

Dear Diary,

After three consecutive days of embarrassing fails, I was ready to throw in the towel. But my managers convinced me to try one last desperate move - flattery. "Compliment is the food of love", they said. And in politics, love directly translates to votes. So armed with a pocketful of appreciative notes, I visited a community leader known to influence many swing voters. "You have the face of an angel" I gushed while handing him a handwritten poem. He seemed quite pleased. Next, I told an elderly voter "Aunty you don't look a day over 50, secret of youth please!" She blushed. I was on a flattering roll. By evening, I had showered praises on dozens - from charming smiles to inspiring leadership. It felt fake but the reactions were good. Everyone left with a smile, and maybe just maybe, a vote for me. My managers say first impressions are everything, and I surely left one. Fingers crossed this brown-nosing actually works! Politics is all about sucking up it seems.

Day 5 of Campaigning

Dear Diary,

Election results day is nearing and the mind games have begun. Rival Ambarish organised a massive roadshow today while I was busy at another rally. Apparently his vehicles and banners dominated every street corner in the city. My campaign has been more "follywood" with random mishaps, but at least people are talking - whether in admiration or amusement. My managers assured me any publicity is good publicity. But I can't help feeling anxious. To destress, I treated myself to a lavish meal featuring all my favourite indulgences. Big mistake, as I have been feeling very bloated and gassy since. Just when I thought the day couldn't get any worse, I bumped into Ambarish at a local market. He smirked and said "I hope you're enjoying your last days of relaxation before conceding defeat". I was seething inside but had to keep up appearances. "The battle is not over yet my friend. May the best man win", I smiled through gritted teeth. Election day is nearing and the mind games have only begun! Politics is a cutthroat world I tell you. Wish me luck in these final moments diary. The thrilling climax awaits!

Year 2050

It was the year 2050 and the environment was in big trouble. The temperature kept risin' like Steven Seagal's chins and animal species were goin' extinct faster than the Kardashians' brain cells. All the scientists kept warnin' the politicians about climate change but all they cared about was the big bucks from the oil tycoons.

The polar bears could no longer be found anywhere near the North Pole cuz the ice caps had melted into ice tea. Florida was almost completely underwater and Spring Break was now held in Antarctica! The Amazon rainforest was cut down to make way for mega cattle farms and beef was the only thing brasileiros could eat. Koalas were now homeless and hangin' around the streets of Sydney tryna get their eucalyptus fix. It was lookin' real grim for Mother Nature.

But then somethin' unexpected happened. The politicians, who were as useful as an ashtray on a motorcycle, finally grew a spine (even though it was covered in oil stains). They realized the environment was a lost cause so they decided to stop tryna "save" it. All the restrictions on pollutin' industries were lifted and big companies were allowed to do as they pleased.

The auto industry was allowed to make gas guzzlers with 50 mpg efficiency and coal power plants popped up everywhere you looked, belchin' smoke that could give Godzilla asthma. Plastic straws made a comeback and single use plastics flooded the markets again. It was an industrial free for all!

And that's when things started lookin' up! With no environmental policies holdin' em back, companies could focus on makin' profits without a care in the world. New jobs were created as industries expanded and the economy started boomin' like Mount St. Helens. Unemployment dropped to 0% as even monks and nuns had to get jobs to pay the bills. With money flowin' freely, people had cash to spend on useless junk they didn't need. Malls, shops and Amazon were rakin' it in as consumerism reached fever pitch. Happy meals now came with a side of plastic toys to choke on.

But the best part was, with the environment in the gutter, scientists now had somethin' new to study. Research fundin' poured in as they tried to find new ways to reverse the damage. Electric cars were upgraded to run on cow farts instead of batteries. New technologies emerged including an inhaler that filtered microplastics from the lungs. Someone even invented an umbrella that protected you from acid rain and global warmin'. With lots of problems to solve, innovation was at an all time high. Even Elon Musk was stumped!

As the years rolled by, a miraculous thing started happenin'. All the pollution we pumped into the atmosphere eventually bounced back the other way and the climate started to stabilize. The greenhouse gases formed a layer like a giant burrito wrap around Earth, trapping in heat like those Snuggies you see infomercials hawkin' at 3am. Glaciers and ice caps began to slowly reform and polar bears were spotted doin' the conga on ice floes once more. Forests replanted themselves with all the extra CO_2 in the air. Animals evolved gills and webbed feet to adapt to rising sea levels.

By 2080, the environment had completely recovered. The air was as toxic as LA smog, rivers had evolved into sludge and trees grew plastic rings like dendrochronologists' dreams. But nature found a way as it always does. Scientists were stunned! It turned out a little pollution was good for the planet - too much cleaning up was suffocating Mother Nature. Who would've thunk it?!

So in the end, by ignorin' climate change and letting industries run wild, we accidental-like saved the environment AND fixed the economy. Everyone was happy, prosperous and chokin' on toxic fumes. It just goes to show that the best solutions are sometimes the most unexpected. Sometimes you gotta take two steps back before you can move forward if you know what I'm sayin. The moral of the story? Don't fix what ain't broke!

The Tale of Two Slanguists

Bangshi Babu was sitting on the couch mindlessly scrolling through his Facebook feed. He had no idea what any of the posts meant since all his friends and family used so many weird slangs and abbreviations in their status updates and comments.

"Lol wbu SMH this weather today IG TBH I'm DEAD," read one such cryptic comment on his sister's selfie. Bangshi scratched his greying hair in confusion. "What in the world are they even talking about?" he muttered to himself.

Just then his son Shibu walked into the living room with his headphones on, eyes glued to his phone screen as usual. "Hey kid, can you please decode what all these abbreviations mean your aunt used in her comment? I'm too old for this modern lingo," pleaded Bangshi.

Shibu took a quick look and laughed. "Dad you're so OOTL. Here's the translation: Lol (laughing out loud) wbu (what about you) SMH (shaking my head) this weather today IG (I guess) TBH (to be honest) I'm DEAD (it's really funny)."

Bangshi's eyes grew wide in wonder. "So much meaning packed into such small words! Your generation has truly revolutionised communication. But how will you old folks like me ever keep up?"

Shibu gave his dad a patronising look. "Dad calm your Jets. You just gotta open your mind and go with the flow. I'll teach you all the essential slangs so you can fLEX on your Facebook friends too."

And so began Bangshi's journey to become a proficient slanguist under Shibu's guidance. Every afternoon after school, Shibu would give his father "slang lessons" where he introduced new acronyms and explained their contextual usages.

In no time at all, Bangshi had mastered common ones like LOL, TMI, BRB, IDK, SMH, etc. He was even throwing around more millennial phrases like "big mood", "same", "yeet" effortlessly in conversations.

One weekend, Bangshi decided to take his newfound slang skills to the next level. He hatched an elaborate plan that was sure to make Shibu proud. On Sunday evening, he announced to the family - "I'm headed to the store real quick, anyone need anything?"

As usual, everyone started listing out their items. But Bangshi had other motives. Once everyone was done, he dropped the bombshell - "Aight fam imma head out, stay safe and don't do anything I wouldn't do! Peace!"

The whole family sat stunned for a moment, trying to process Bangshi's outburst in millennial. Shibu was the first to react - "No way, is that my dad?! Someone pinch me I must be dreaming! What a massive power move, I think I just caught second hand cool."

The slang lessons had paid off - Bangshi had successfully established himself as the resident "cool dad" of the house with that one power-packed statement. Word of his prowess spread far and wide through friends and relatives. Soon everyone wanted the secret to Bangshi's slanguistic skills.

Little did they know, behind the scenes Bangshi and Shibu were scheming even bigger. They decided to collaborate on a book - "Slang for Dummies: An Idiot's Guide to Sounding Lit AF". Thanks to Bangshi'snatural wit and Shibu's editing, the book was an instant bestseller.

Overnight, Bangshi became the most sought after motivational speaker at schools and colleges. His talks on "Embracing Modern Lingo" left audiences in splits. Not just India, soon he was touring internationally and amassing millions of followers on social media.

Father and son had proven that with the right blend of old and new, anyone can go from BOOMER to ZOOMER. Their message resonated far and wide - slang knows no age, so don't be basic, get lit fam!

How to Procrastinate?

It was a sunny Saturday morning and Karan was still tucked in his bed. As the sunlight peeked through the curtains, Karan stretched and yawned. He opened his eyes and stared at the ceiling, lost in his thoughts.

"Ugh, I have that project due tomorrow about how we spend our weekends. I still haven't even started it!" Karan thought to himself. He knew he should get up and start working on it but the bed was just too cozy. Five more minutes, he told himself.

Just then, Karan heard his mom calling him for breakfast. "Coming!" he shouted as he reluctantly got off the bed. During breakfast, his mom asked, "Don't you have a project to submit tomorrow? You better get started after this."

Karan knew she was right but he wasn't in the mood to work yet. After breakfast, he lounged on the sofa and turned the TV on. As he aimlessly channel surfed, an idea suddenly struck him. "What if I wrote about procrastination for my project? It is kind of how I'm spending my weekend after all!" Karan exclaimed.

Excited about his new plan, Karan got his laptop and started writing. He wrote about how procrastination is actually productive in its own way. He filled pages with personal anecdotes and experiences where waiting till the last minute sparked unexpected creativity. Soon, he was so into his work that he didn't even realize time flying by. By evening, he had finished a draft.

The next day at school, Karan wasn't feeling stressed about the deadline at all. In fact, he couldn't stop smiling as he handed the project to his teacher, Mr. Souvik. During the presentation later that day, Karan won over the class with his unique perspective on procrastination. Even Mr. Souvik was impressed.

"You know, the student might be onto something with this procrastination idea. I sometimes find that waiting till the last minute inspires me too," thought Souvik. That weekend, Souvik couldn't stop procrastinating on grading his students work. On Sunday night, with a huge stack of papers left to grade, Souvik got an idea.

"Why don't I turn this procrastination into productivity by writing a research paper on procrastination? I can use examples from popular culture and get student perspectives too. And I can meet this grading deadline in the process!" decided Souvik. Fueled by motivation, Souvik graded non-stop and also penned down his research in between.

By Monday morning, Souvik had not only finished grading but also completed a draft of the research paper. He was pleased with his results and proud of himself for channelling procrastination so well. In class that day, Souvik shared copies of his research with the students and informed them about an upcoming district level paper presentation competition.

"Since the topic involves student perspectives, I think Karan should represent our class and school," suggested Souvik. Karan was thrilled at the idea. With Souvik's guidance and feedback, Karan polished his presentation skills. To their surprise, Karan ended up winning the competition with his passion-filled speech on productive procrastination.

Karan's success inspired many students to embrace procrastination. Slowly this became a regular phenomena in the school. Deadlines which were previously dreaded now sparked new ideas and quality work. Teachers began setting dates deliberately close to the events, anticipating well-written lesson plans and assignments at the last minute.

Word of this school's procrastination phenomenon spread far and wide. Education experts from around the globe came to study this unique approach. Within a few years, productive procrastination was adopted in schools worldwide. By high school graduation, Karan's initial insight had revolutionized the education system and completely changed society's views on deadlines and last minute work. And it all started because Karan cleverly turned his procrastination into a winning project!

The Daily Grind

Shukhen stretched and yawned loudly as the morning sunlight drifted through the blinds in his small apartment bedroom. It was 6am and time to start another day of the daily grind. As much as he enjoyed his boring 9-5 office job, the highlight of Shukhen's day was the adventure that awaited him on his morning commute - a wild ride on the local public train.

While most people dreaded being stuck on a crowded, germ-infested train with strange smells and noises, Shukhen looked forward to the mystery and mayhem that could unfold before him each morning. He popped a piece of gum in his mouth for freshness and grabbed his battered briefcase before heading out the door. "Time for the fun to begin!" he said to himself with a smirk.

The train station was a zoo as usual with hustling and bustling people shoving to board the packed carriages. Shukhen squeezed his way onto the crowded car and gripped a dirty overhead strap for balance. As the train jerked forward, he surveyed his car-mates - there was Crazy Mike the conspiracy theorist yelling about 5G mind control chips, Hungover Helen close to vomiting in her coffee cup, and Smelly Steve passing gas without a care. It was going to be a hot mess of a ride as always.

Halfway to the city, the train came to a screeching halt and the lights flickered off, leaving the passengers in darkness. "Not again!" sighed Shukhen. But for him, this was the most exciting part - you never knew what drama might unfold in the enclosed space without rules or restrictions. A fight broke out a few rows back over an accidental butt grab in the chaos. Shukhen watched with glee as the combatants rolled around on the dirty floor pulling hair and throwing wild punches.

Eventually the lights flickered back on to reveal the bloody and battered brawlers being detained by transit guards. "Just another morning on the rails!" thought Shukhen. But the action wasn't over yet. The next stop, a paranoid schizophrenic rushed on screaming about government spies before projectile vomiting all over the place. Total pandemonium! Shukhen was loving every minute of the insanity.

By the time he reached his downtown stop, Shukhen's boring office job seemed like a welcome break from the wild ride of public transit adventures. But he knew another thrill-packed commute awaited him that evening. As he exited the train car, he couldn't help but smile at the thought of what exciting nonsense the ride home might bring. While others saw public transport as a necessary evil, for Shukhen it was modern day thrill-seeking at its best. The daily grind was never so entertaining!

Ghosted

I can't believe Jessica just ghosted me like that. After all we had been through - the latte dates, Netflix and chill sessions, the clumsy hand holding - poof! Gone without a trace. I should have seen the signs - when she stopped "hearting" my Instagram selfies and took three hours to reply to my "wyd" texts.

I was devastated. How could she do this to me, Rajdeep, King of Corny Pickup Lines and Self-Deprecating Humor? Doesn't she know she'll never find another guy as quirky and one-of-a-kind as me?

In my sorrow, I took to my bed for three days straight, listening to depressing Taylor Swift albums on repeat and browsing her Facebook profile way more than is healthy. By day four, my Cheetos stash was depleted and I was starting to smell funky. It was time to wallow in self-pity out in the real world.

On my first outing, I ran into Jessica's friend Jane at the frozen yogurt place. "Oh hey Raj, I'm so sorry to hear about you and Jess. Maybe it just wasn't meant to be," she said, patting my shoulder awkwardly. I saw my chance for some closure.

"Jane please, I need answers. Did she say anything about me? Am I too much of a goofball? Not romantic enough? Does she have a new man already?" Jane grimaced. "I shouldn't say anything, but between you and me, she said the pet names got weird and you quoted The Office one too many times."

Ouch, straight to the feelings. At least I had my raison d'être for being ghosted. It was time to make some changes, starting with clearing out my buzzword bingo board vocabulary. No more dropping "big moods" or forcing "Same hat!" into conversations. I was going to reinvent myself into the kind of guy a girl would be PROUD to couple up with.

First up - upgrading my look. Out with the graphic tees and stubbly facial hair. In with fitted button-ups, tortoise shell glasses and a sharp fade. The hipsters at the local coffee shop did a double take when I strode in looking like a Calvin Klein model.

Next was expanding my interests beyond superhero movies and Fortnite. I listened to podcasts about current events while I worked out, hit up art galleries on the weekends, and read enough to have Opinions on books. No more being "that Netflix guy" - I was now well-rounded Raj, full of conversation starters.

The final frontier was improving my communication skills. I traded in clunky "wyd" texts for thoughtful check-ins and regularly asked friends deep questions to understand them better. When interacting with prospective dates, I listened actively without interrupting and gave reassuring affirmations rather than distracting stories about myself.

It wasn't easy changing my whole persona after 26 years of being One Way, but I knew it was for the best. After a few months of self-improvement, I noticed the positive changes all around me - more invitations from pals, matches who wanted to meet IRL, and people generally seeking me out more.

It was then that fate dropped Jessica back into my life. We ran into each other at a party and after an awkward greeting, she said "Raj, I barely recognize you! You seem so put together and...grown up? What happened to you?" I laughed. "Funny story, being ghosted by you was the wake up call I needed. I hope we can be friends." She grinned. "I'd like that."

In the end, getting ghosted by Jessica was the best thing that ever happened to me. It lit a fire to better myself and now I'm a whole new, evolving person. Who would've thought getting blown off could be so life-changing? I sure learned more from my L than any success. Thanks for the lesson, Jess - you may have disappeared but your influence will remain.

Interview

My name is Raman and I just flew all the way from Mumbai, India to New York City for my very first job interview with BigShot Inc., a huge tech company. I was super nervous as I dressed in the only suit I packed and studied all the typical interview questions Americans ask.

After getting lost in the subway twice, I finally arrived at the skyscraper BigShot Inc. was located in. The lobby looked fancier than any office I've seen back home. There were couches, plants and a fancy water cooler. As I waited for my interview, I overheard conversations in perfect English flying by about projects, deadlines and quarterly goals.

When I was called into the conference room, there were three intimidating interviewers staring back at me. "Hi Raman, thanks for coming in. Tell us a bit about yourself" said the bald dude sitting in the middle.

"Well uh...my name is Raman. I'm from Mumbai but just moved to the city. I have a masters in computer science from IIT Bombay. I really like coding and building apps. That's pretty much me in a nutshell!" I said with a big cheesy grin, hoping they would find my awkwardness charming.

The lady on the left chimed in "That's great Raman but can you tell us about any relevant work experience? What projects have you worked on?"

Uh oh, I should have seen this question coming. The truth was I didn't have any real work experience besides some school projects and freelancing on Fiverr. I had to think fast.

"Well you see, in India we don't really do internships like you guys. But I have worked on some really groundbreaking stuff. I once made a calorie counting app for cows that was such a hit, it was featured on Indian TikTok. The cows loved it! I also may have technically invented WhatsApp...but Zuckerberg stole my idea."

The interviewers exchanged confused looks. Crap, I think I went too far with that WhatsApp thing. The bald dude spoke up again "While those projects sound very...interesting, we're really looking for more traditional work experiences here. Can you tell us about any past roles or responsibilities you held?"

I was sweating profusely now. I had to pull something out of my butt fast. "You're absolutely right, apologies. I actually used to intern at TCS here in New York awhile back. I led a team that developed some machine learning algorithms to detect fraud for Chase bank. It was challenging but very rewarding. We saved them millions!"

More awkward silence. These people were too smart to fall for my B.S. The lady on the left cut to the chase. "I'm sorry Raman but we have no record of you ever working for TCS or Chase. Is there anything real you can share about your background?"

I was screwed. There was no twisting the truth anymore, they had seen right through me. I had to come clean.

"You got me, I'm so sorry to have wasted your time. The truth is I don't have any real work experience. All my skills are just from school projects. I know I'm not qualified for this role but I'm a fast learner and a hard worker. Please give me a chance, I really want to prove myself."

The interviewers consulted quietly among themselves. I sat there sweating bullets, waiting for the axe to drop. Finally, the bald dude spoke up.

"Raman, we appreciate your honesty. While you may not have the experiences we're looking for right now, I see a lot of potential in you. How would you feel about starting as an unpaid intern here for 3 months?

If you can show us your skills and work ethic, we may be able to bring you on properly after."

I couldn't believe it! They were offering me a chance, all I had to do was work my tail off to prove myself. I enthusiastically accepted right away.

As I excitedly left the building, I felt hopeful. Sure the interview didn't go as planned, but I got my big break. It might take some time, but BigShot Inc. would see my worth. This was only the beginning - just wait until they see what I can really do!

About the Author

Sayan Panda

Sayan Panda, a talented author hailing from the vibrant city of Kolkata, has captivated readers with his imaginative storytelling. With a background in English literature and a passion for the written word, Panda has established himself as a noteworthy voice in the literary world. Having already published eight books across various genres, he now ventures into unexplored territory, delving into the realms of the comic and the satire. This foray into the satirical and fun showcases Panda's versatile storytelling abilities and his willingness to push the boundaries of his craft. Alongside his writing endeavors, Panda also dedicates himself to educating young minds as a dedicated school teacher.

www.ingramcontent.com/pod-product-compliance
Lightning Source LLC
LaVergne TN
LVHW041638070526
838199LV00052B/3434